Park Avenue School
Title I

Sojourner Truth's

Ain't I a Woman?

a play adaptation

Ohio Women's Rights Convention of 1851

On May 28, 1851, hundreds of people crowded into a church in Akron, Ohio, to attend a women's rights convention. At the time, women in the United States had far fewer rights and opportunities than men. Women could not vote or hold political office. They were barred from certain careers and were usually paid less than men. If a woman was married, her husband controlled her earnings and property. The goal of the 1851 Ohio Women's Rights Convention—like other meetings that women had organized over the previous three years—was to discuss this unfair situation and find ways to reform it. Few could have predicted that the gathering in Akron would be the occasion for one of the greatest speeches in American history.

By 1851, slavery, which was outlawed in the North but legal in the South, had become the most controversial issue in the country. Anti-slavery advocates, or abolitionists, wanted to get rid of slavery completely. As the country expanded westward in the 1840s, many Northerners wanted to ban slavery in the new territories. Other Northerners, however, opposed abolitionists, fearing their ideas would upset white Southerners and threaten national unity. These opponents often disrupted abolitionist meetings and attacked speakers.

Frances Dana Gage

One abolitionist who strongly supported women's rights was writer and lecturer Frances Dana Gage, chairperson of the 1851 Ohio Women's Rights Convention. Gage welcomed everyone to the convention, both women and men, as well as those who favored and opposed women's rights. On May 29, 1851, the second day of the convention, some male speakers denounced women's rights and criticized women as inferior to men. At this point, a tall black woman—the only African American in the audience—stood up and walked to the front of the room. Her name was Sojourner Truth. Truth spoke briefly, unplanned and unrehearsed, questioning the men who had just belittled women's rights. The words she uttered became one of the most memorable speeches of the nineteenth century—but not until Gage recounted them in an article she wrote twelve years later.

Abolitionist and feminist Frances Dana Gage presided over the 1851 Ohio Women's Rights Convention where Sojourner Truth delivered her "Ain't I a Woman?" speech.

Ain't I a Woman?

by Sojourner Truth

Well, children, where there is so much racket there must be something out of kilter. I think that 'twixt the negroes of the South and the women at the North, all talking about rights, the white men will be in a fix pretty soon. But what's all this here talking about?

That man over there says that women need to be helped into carriages, and lifted over ditches, and to have the best place everywhere. Nobody ever helps me into carriages, or over mud-puddles, or gives me any best place! And ain't I a woman? Look at me! Look at my arm! I have ploughed and planted, and gathered into barns, and no man could head me! And ain't I a woman? I could work as much and eat as much as a man—when I could get it—and bear the lash as well! And ain't I a woman? I have borne thirteen children, and seen most all sold off to slavery, and when I cried out with my mother's grief, none but Jesus heard me. And ain't I a woman?

Then they talk about this thing in the head; what's this they call it? [member of the audience whispers, "intellect."] That's right, honey. What's that got to do with women's rights or negroes' rights? If my cup won't hold but a pint, and yours holds a quart, wouldn't you be mean not to let me have my little half measure full?

Then that little man in black there, he says women can't have as much rights as men, 'cause Christ wasn't a woman! Where did your Christ come from? Where did your Christ come from? From God and a woman! Man had nothing to do with Him.

If the first woman God ever made was strong enough to turn the world upside down all alone, these women together ought to be able to turn it back, and get it right side up again! And now they are asking to do it, the men better let them.

Obliged to you for hearing me, and now old Sojourner ain't got nothing more to say.

Rhetoric and Refrain

Sojourner Truth could neither read nor write, but she was skilled in rhetoric, the art of speaking persuasively. She makes this speech memorable by repeating, "ain't I a woman?" a number of times. Each time she asks this question, she makes her point stronger. A recurring phrase such as this is called a refrain.

Name: Sojourner Truth

Born: around 1797

Died: November 26, 1883

Hometown: Ulster County, New York

Early Years: Sojourner Truth began her life as a slave named Isabella Baumfree. When New York abolished slavery in 1827, Isabella became free. She went to court to regain custody of a son who had been sold by her former owner. Later, she moved to New York City and worked as a housekeeper, servant, and cook. She also became a preacher. In 1843, she changed her name to Sojourner Truth. Although she was unable to read or write, she spoke eloquently. In her speeches, she attacked slavery and recounted her life story. She transfixed audiences everywhere. In 1850, she dictated her memoirs and had them published. Her book became a best seller. She sold it at conventions as she traveled around the country on behalf of abolition and women's rights.

Famous Works: *The Narrative of Sojourner Truth* (1850); various speeches including "Address to the First Annual Meeting of the American Equal Rights Association" (1867)

Famous Quotes: "I can't read a book, but I can read de people." "Dere's nothin' like standin' up for yer rights!"

Interesting Fact: Truth visited President Lincoln at the White House during the Civil War. She gave him a photograph of herself, and he showed her a Bible that African Americans of Baltimore had recently given him as a gift. How strange, Truth commented, that just a few years before it would have been against the law in many states for black people to have learned how to read that very book.

Ain't I a Woman?

CAST OF CHARACTERS

in order of appearance

Frances Gage, 1863
feminist and abolitionist writer

Lucinda
young ex-slave

Mrs. Johnson
suffragist and assistant to Frances Gage

Frances Gage, 1851
president of the 1851 Ohio Women's Rights Convention

Maisie Thompkins
attendee of the 1851 Ohio Women's Rights Convention

Jebediah Fairweather
attendee of the 1851 Ohio Women's Rights Convention

Minister Soames
local minister in Akron, Ohio

Minister Bagley
local minister in Akron, Ohio

Sojourner Truth
abolitionist, ex-slave, traveling preacher

SETTING

Frances Gage's drawing room in 1863;
a church in Akron, Ohio, in 1851

Frances Gage, 1863: Dear reader, I write this article to you in the year 1863. It is an article about Sojourner Truth, the traveling preacher who made history at the 1851 Ohio Women's Rights Convention in Akron. My name is Frances Gage. I was the president of that convention, and I can tell you that it was my extreme pleasure to meet such an incredible human being. She was a tall, dignified ex-slave who traveled all around our great nation, speaking out against injustices like slavery and inequality for women. And when she spoke out at the Women's Rights Convention, you better believe people listened! So return with me now to the city of Akron in the year 1851. I guarantee you will find it a truly amazing moment in history!

Lucinda: Mrs. Gage, ma'am, we're gonna need more chairs and tables for all the people who have come to the convention.

Mrs. Johnson: It's so exciting, Frances! The church is filled to overflowing. The volunteers are wearing out their shoe leather passing out booklets and posters to everyone.

Frances Gage, 1851: Splendid. If all turns out well, this could be one of our most successful women's rights conventions!

Mrs. Johnson: I certainly hope so, Frances. I see many of the townsfolk, and people are coming in from the countryside by droves. Here comes the Widow Thompkins—I can't believe she took time off from working at her farm—she's got no husband to help her. Hi there, Maisie!

Maisie Thompkins: Hi there yourself, Mrs. Johnson. Say, Lucinda, are these itty bitty chairs the only things you've got to sit on? To put it bluntly, I'm not a little girl.

Lucinda: Oh, goodness no, those won't work at all. I'll go see if I can get you a sturdier chair, Widow Thompkins.

Jebediah Fairweather: I'll take care of that, Lucinda. Here you go, Maisie. I held on to this chair for you because I hoped you'd be coming into town for this meeting.

Maisie Thompkins: Yes, this chair is very comfortable. Thank you so much, Jebediah.

Jebediah Fairweather: My pleasure, Maisie. It's the least I can do since you've allowed my farm to have access to your water well. We've all got to help one another, right?

Mrs. Johnson: Oh dear, Frances!

Frances Gage, 1851: What's wrong?

Mrs. Johnson: There's a Negro woman who's just come into the convention hall. It's Sojourner Truth, the outspoken abolitionist!

Frances Gage, 1851: What's wrong with speaking out against slavery? It's everyone's natural right to want freedom, and everyone's duty to speak up for it.

Mrs. Johnson: This is neither the proper time nor place, Frances. We need as much support for women's rights as we can get. If Sojourner Truth starts talking about freeing the slaves, people will forget all about women's rights, and things might get ugly in here.

Frances Gage, 1863: I wish I could say that Mrs. Johnson was worrying needlessly, but she wasn't. Even back then, in 1851, the mention of slavery was enough to start a fight. Now we are in 1863. The civil war that our country has been fighting for the past two years is largely about slavery.

Minister Soames: Look at that colored woman who just came into the church hall, Minister Bagley! I knew it! It's bad enough that this meeting is about women's rights, but now we're going to have to listen to some Negro busybody talking about ending slavery!

Minister Bagley: Don't worry, Minister Soames. With all the arguments we're going to put forth *against* women's rights, we'll stop this convention before anyone ever gets to talking about freeing the slaves!

Lucinda: Psst! Are you Ms. Sojourner Truth, ma'am?

Sojourner Truth: That I am, child. And what's your name?

Lucinda: My name is Lucinda, ma'am. Please don't take this the wrong way, but I'm just tellin' you for your own safety that maybe you shouldn't be at the convention today. A lot of people seem to have somethin' against you. I just thought you should know.

Sojourner Truth: I 'preciate your concern, Lucinda, but how will anything ever change if we don't speak up? Now, don't fret yourself, girl. Here, take this book—it tells the story of my life. Can you read?

Lucinda: *(proudly)* Yes, ma'am!

Sojourner Truth: Good. When you read what's in this book, you'll understand why I don't worry about what these people think of me.

Lucinda: Thank you, ma'am. And please be careful.

Mrs. Johnson: Please don't let Sojourner Truth speak, Frances! Every newspaper in the land will have our cause mixed up with abolition and no one will take us suffragettes seriously.

Frances Gage, 1851: We shall see when the time comes. I think it's time to start the meeting. *(at the podium)* May I have your attention, everyone? Thank you. Hello, ladies and gentlemen. Thank you for coming. My name is Frances Gage, and I'm a feminist, which means I fight for the rights of women. Things are not easy for women right now. We don't have the right to vote, and if we are married, we don't have the right to own property. Men believe us to be naturally weak and frightened, and they think we are not capable of thinking for ourselves. But nothing could be further from the truth. We can be strong and fearless, and we deserve to be respected by men. But even more important than respect, we deserve the rights and privileges that men possess—

Minister Bagley: Stuff and nonsense!

Frances Gage, 1851: I beg your pardon?

Minister Bagley: I said, stuff and nonsense! I demand a rebuttal!

Frances Gage, 1851: If you would be so kind as to approach the pulpit and identify yourself, sir, you may have your rebuttal—your chance to speak.

Minister Bagley: I am Minister Bagley, and I am appalled at having to listen to this nonsense about men not respecting women! Ladies, we do respect you—very much!

Jebediah Fairweather and **Minister Soames:** Here, here!

Minister Soames: (*addressing the crowd*) But surely you must see that women, the fairer sex, are weaker by nature. You don't have the strength to do the types of strenuous, backbreaking work that we men can do easily. You are delicate beings, as fragile as the petals of a flower, and you deserve to be cherished and protected. That is why we help you into your carriages, lift you over ditches, and make sure you have all the best places to live. You are the reason we toil so hard at our jobs, because we know we have the responsibility for providing for your well-being at all times.

Jebediah Fairweather and **Minister Bagley:** Here, here!

Maisie Thompkins: Excuse me, may I say something? Now that I'm a widow, I alone have the responsibility for providing for myself and my—

Minister Bagley: But just as we have that responsibility to provide for you, you have the responsibility to obey us, and to accept that we, as men, are superior to you—physically, intellectually, and spiritually.

Mrs. Johnson: Excuse me, sir. I don't mean to disagree with you, but how can you say that men are superior to women in all things—

Minister Soames: *(interrupting)* —And don't forget, Bagley, that women also have a responsibility to brighten our world with beauty and grace—not to pollute the air with ungrateful cries of—dare I even say those foul words—women's rights!

Minister Soames and **Minister Bagley:** Down with women's rights! Down with women's rights!

Mrs. Johnson: Now, see here—

Minister Bagley: Any man who disagrees is less than a man, and any woman who disagrees is no God-fearing woman!

Minister Soames: Well said, sir. She's no woman worth knowing at all, Bagley!

Jebediah Fairweather, Minister Soames, and **Minister Bagley:** Down with women's rights! Down with women's rights!

Francis Gage, 1863: Dear reader, things had gotten very tense. Some of the men in attendance began disrupting the meeting with jeers and shouts and nasty remarks. The ministers were getting the men so agitated that the women were afraid to speak.

Minister Bagley: Even the Bible says we men are better than women! The first human being, after all, was Adam—a man. And who got that man kicked out of the Garden of Eden? A woman, of course—his wife Eve. And all because, like you women here today, she didn't know her place!

Jebediah Fairweather and **Minister Soames:** Put the women back in their place! Put the women back in their place!

Minister Bagley: Jesus Christ was the only human being who had God as a father. If that doesn't demonstrate the superiority of man, I don't know what does.

Jebediah Fairweather and **Minister Soames:** Here, here!

Jebediah Fairweather, Minister Soames, and **Minister Bagley:** Down with women's rights! Down with women's rights!

Frances Gage, 1851: *(to the disorderly crowd)* Order! Order, please! *(quietly to Mrs. Johnson)* Mrs. Johnson, there's got to be a woman out there who can argue against these speeches. Because if no one speaks up, our cause is doomed. *(to crowd)* These ministers have made some very strong speeches, and I thank them for sharing their opinions. Now, is there anyone out there who would like to respond for the women's cause? *(silence)* No one at all?

Sojourner Truth: I'll speak.

Frances Gage, 1851: Who said that? I can't see who said that.

Sojourner Truth: *(standing)* That's mighty unusual, ma'am, 'cause I'm kinda hard to miss.

Jebediah Fairweather: Goodness gracious! That's the tallest Negro woman I've ever seen!

Maisie Thompkins: That's the tallest woman I've ever seen, period!

Frances Gage, 1863: Sojourner was indeed tall and also thin. She was in her fifties at the time, but she was as fit as someone much younger. On the day of the convention, she wore a simple gray dress. Upon her head was a white turban—a white turban, mind you, with a sunbonnet on top of that!

Jebediah Fairweather: That's some mighty unusual headgear!

Maisie Thompkins: Hush up, Jebediah!

Frances Gage, 1851: Would you be so kind as to introduce yourself, ma'am?

Sojourner Truth: My name is Truth, Ms. Sojourner Truth.

Mrs. Johnson: (*whispering*) Oh please, Frances, don't let her speak! If you think the meeting is getting out of hand now, just wait until the issue of slavery comes up!

Frances Gage, 1851: America is the land of the free and the home of the brave, Mrs. Johnson. If anyone is brave enough to come up here and talk about being free, I'm brave enough to let them. (*to Sojourner Truth*) The floor is yours, Ms. Truth, for as long as you want it.

Minister Bagley: I can't believe she's letting that woman speak.

Minister Soames: Bide your time, Bagley. We'll put that troublemaker in her place.

Frances Gage, 1863: There was tension in the air as everyone watched Sojourner walk regally, like a queen, up the aisle of the church. She took her place at the pulpit, sang briefly to herself, then spoke.

Sojourner Truth: Thank you, Mrs. Gage. *(addressing the crowd)* Well, children, there's so much racket here, somethin' must be out of kilter. You've got the black folks in the South talkin' 'bout their rights and you've got the women in the North talkin' 'bout theirs. So now I ask you, what's all the talkin' 'bout? Well, let me start with this man right here. *(pointing to Minister Soames)* He's sayin' that women need to be helped into carriages, and lifted over ditches, and have the best place everywhere. Is that right, mister?

Minister Soames: Yes, that's right.

Sojourner Truth: Well, nobody's ever helped me any place. And ain't I a woman?

Minister Soames: Um . . . well . . . yes, I would have to say . . . yes.

Sojourner Truth: Mmm-hmm. And take a look at my arm. *(flexing the muscles of one arm)* Come on now, look at it.

Jebediah Fairweather: I believe she's got more muscle than you, Minister Soames!

Minister Soames: She's got more muscle than me and Bagley combined, Jebediah!

Sojourner Truth: If I've got more muscle than you, I've gotten it from plowin', plantin', and gatherin' bushels of crops into barns. No man did it for me. And ain't I a woman?

Maisie Thompkins: (*standing*) You are, Ms. Truth, and you're not the only one! (*to crowd*) For the past three years, ever since I've been a widow, I've had to do all the chores on my farm by myself, not to mention take care of my children! Keep on telling the truth, Ms. Truth!

Lucinda and **Mrs. Johnson:** Keep on telling the truth, Ms. Truth!

Sojourner Truth: I could work as much, and eat as much as any man—(*chuckling*) well, that is, when I could get it. And I've had to bear the slave driver's lash as well! And ain't I a woman?

Lucinda: She's not the only one who's had to deal with that, either. I've got the scars on my back to prove it! And I'm not afraid to speak about it anymore, Ms. Truth! Keep on tellin' the truth!

Sojourner Truth: I have borne children and seen most of them sold into slavery, and when I cried out with a mother's grief, none but Jesus heard me. And ain't I a woman?

Lucinda, Mrs. Johnson, Frances Gage, 1851, and **Maisie Thompkins:** (*cheering and clapping*) Keep on telling the truth, Ms. Truth!

Minister Soames: (*loudly*) This is all very touching, Ms. Truth, but the fact remains that women do not have the intellect of a man so they do not deserve the rights and privileges of a man!

Sojourner Truth: (*whispering to Mrs. Gage*) What's that word mean, *intellect*?

Frances Gage, 1851: *(whispering back) Intellect* means "the knowledge people have in their heads."

Sojourner Truth: Oh. Okay. Thank you, honey. *(to Minister Soames)* Mister, what on Earth has intellect got to do with women's rights, or black folks' rights, or anybody's rights? If my cup won't hold but a pint and yours holds a quart, wouldn't you be mean not to let me have my full pint?

Maisie Thompkins: She's right! I want my full pint of rights!

Jebediah Fairweather: Nothing pint-sized about you, Maisie!

Maisie Thompkins: How dare you insult me, Jebediah!

Jebediah Fairweather: I just meant you've got a lot of everything, Maisie, including sense! Come on, woman—I'm on your side. Don't you know that?

Maisie Thompkins: (*giggling*) Oh Jebediah, you're such a caution! But stop chatting with me and start chanting with me!

Jebediah Fairweather: You got it!

Maisie Thompkins and **Jebediah Fairweather:** Up with women's rights! Up with women's rights!

Sojourner Truth: (*pointing to Minister Bagley*) Now, let me get to what that man in black over there said. He believes women can't have as many rights as men 'cause Christ wasn't a woman.

Minister Bagley: That's exactly right—Christ was a man. (*smugly*) Can't deny that, can you, Ms. Truth?

Sojourner Truth: No, I surely can't. But I've got a question for you: Where did your Christ come from?

Minister Bagley: I beg your pardon?

Sojourner Truth: (*shouting*) I said, mister, where did your Christ come from? From God and a woman! Man had nothin' to do with him!

Lucinda: (*cheering*) You got that right!

Minister Soames: (*chuckling*) You've got to admit, Bagley, she does know her Bible.

Minister Bagley: Oh, button your lip, Soames!

Minister Soames: (*shocked*) Bagley!

Sojourner Truth: One last little thing and I'll be through. (*pointing to Minister Bagley*) That man over there said Eve got Adam kicked out of the Garden of Eden. Well, if the first woman God ever made was strong enough to turn the world upside down like that all by herself, then you women together ought to be able to turn it back and get it right-side up again. And men, now that these women are askin' to do just that, you'd better let them!

Minister Soames: Well, I must say—I must say—by golly, you do make sense and a good argument. I think I need to rethink my thinking, Ms. Truth!

Minister Bagley: (*shocked*) Soames, have you lost your mind?

Minister Soames: Not at all. I take my faith very seriously, and I have been listening very closely to this woman—this Ms. Sojourner Truth. She takes her faith very seriously, and she has made a strong case for her cause. I admire that, even as I am astonished by it, for she is an ex-slave who did not have even the limited advantages of a white woman to draw upon.

Minister Bagley: But Soames!

Minister Soames: If a woman from such a background can gain my respect, perhaps it is true that we men have been underestimating all our womenfolk.

Minister Bagley: *But Soames!*

Minister Soames: Oh, button *your* lip, Bagley!

Lucinda, Mrs. Johnson, Frances Gage, 1851, and Maisie Thompkins: Here, here! Up with women's rights! Up with women's rights! Hurrah, Sojourner Truth!

Sojourner Truth: Obliged to you all for hearin' me, and now old Sojourner ain't got nothin' more to say.

Lucinda, Mrs. Johnson, Maisie Thompkins, Jebediah Fairweather, and Minister Soames: (*giving her a standing ovation*) Three cheers for Sojourner Truth! Hurrah, hurrah, hurrah!

Frances Gage, 1863: That final moment is etched indelibly in my mind. Amid roars of applause, Sojourner returned to her corner, leaving more than a few of us with tears streaming down our cheeks and gratitude beating in our hearts. She had taken us up in her strong arms and carried us safely over a muddy swamp of difficulty. She turned the tide in our favor.

Maisie Thompkins: (*sniffling*) Oh, Jebediah! Wasn't that speech moving?

Jebediah Fairweather: It certainly was, Maisie. There, there, take my handkerchief.

Mrs. Johnson: It's amazing, Frances! Sojourner Truth has got all the women, and many of the men, on their feet cheering and stomping and clapping. I wouldn't have believed it if I hadn't seen it myself!

Lucinda: And Mrs. Johnson, surely the newspapers won't say Ms. Truth is a rabble-rouser. Why, she did a great thing today for women's rights!

Mrs. Johnson: Yes, she did, Lucinda. In fact, I can't wait to read about this in the papers. I'm sure it will be a thrilling account.

Lucinda: And I bet I know just what the headline's gonna be!

Lucinda and **Mrs. Johnson:** *(laughing together)* "Ain't I a woman?"

Francis Gage, 1863: And so dear reader, let me conclude by saying that I have never seen anything like the magical influence of Sojourner Truth on that day. Even if my account of the events of that day conveys only some small part of the miracle that was Sojourner Truth, you are truly fortunate. Respectfully yours, Frances D. Gage.

The End

1. Historically, Sojourner Truth was the only African American at the 1851 Ohio Women's Rights Convention. Why do you think the playwright chooses to include Lucinda, a young African American woman and ex-slave? (author's purpose; text-to-text connections)

2. At first, Jebediah Fairweather is against women's rights, but he changes his opinion during the course of the play. Cite two possible reasons for this change. (recall details; make inferences)

3. The word *ain't* used in the title is not proper English. What does this word mean and why is it so powerful in the speech and script? (vocabulary in context; interpretation)

4. The two male ministers in the play supported their argument with opinion, while the women cited facts. Describe these differences and how they impacted the story. (fact vs. opinion; understanding plot)

5. Sojourner Truth's message about women's rights was delivered in 1851, yet today women still do not have all the advantages that men have. Give an example from today. (critical thinking; theme)

6. *Intellect* is defined in the script as "knowledge people have in their heads." How would you define the intellect Sojourner Truth had? (vocabulary; assertion from text; synthesis)

7. Why do you think it took Frances Gage twelve years to write the article about Sojourner Truth's speech? (text-to-world connections; interpretation; inference)